Amazing
Fish

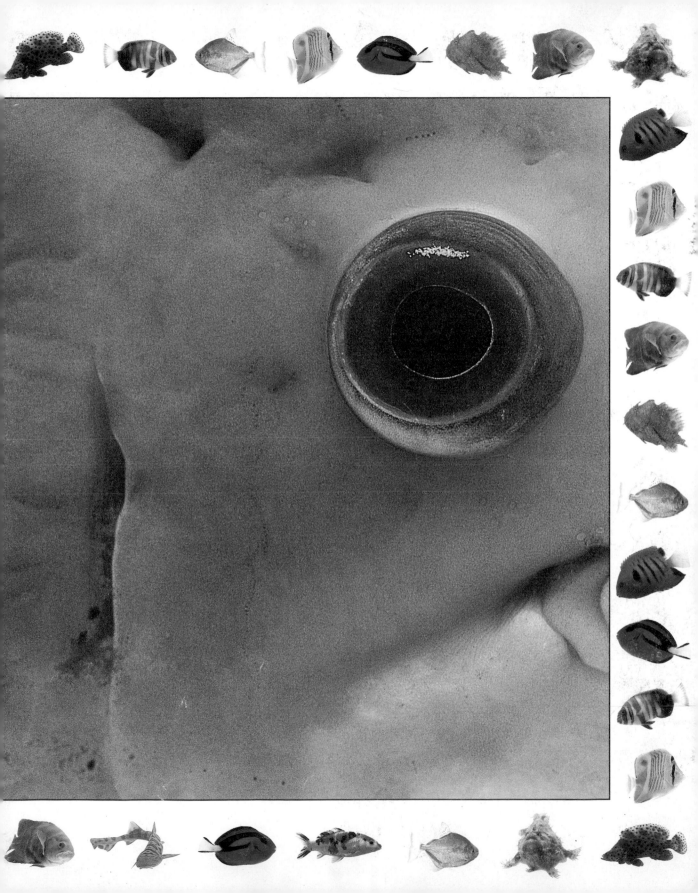

Amazing Fish

WRITTEN BY
MARY LING

PHOTOGRAPHED BY
JERRY YOUNG

ALFRED A. KNOPF • NEW YORK

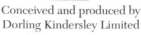

Conceived and produced by
Dorling Kindersley Limited

Project editors Scott Steedman and Louise Pritchard
Art editor Toni Rann
Senior art editor Jacquie Gulliver
Production Louise Barratt

Illustrations by Ruth Lindsay, Ruth Benton, John Hutchinson, and Valerie Price
Animals supplied by Aqua Marine, Maidenhead Aquatics (pp.12 tr, 18-19, 22 tc);
Trevor Smith's Animal World (pp. 22-23)
Editorial consultants The staff of the Natural History Museum, London

This is a Borzoi Book published by Alfred A. Knopf, Inc.

First American edition, 1991

Text copyright © 1991 Dorling Kindersley Limited, London.
Photographs copyright © 1991 to Jerry Young.
All rights reserved under International and Pan-American Copyright Conventions.
Published in the United States by Alfred A. Knopf, Inc., New York.
Distributed by Random House, Inc., New York.
Published in Great Britain by
Dorling Kindersley Limited, London.
Manufactured in Italy   0 9 8 7 6 5

Library of Congress Cataloging in Publication Data
Ling, Mary
Amazing fish/written by Mary Ling;
photographs by Jerry Young.
p.cm. – (Eyewitness juniors)
Summary: Introduces memorable members of the fish world, explains what
makes them unique, and describes important characteristics of the entire group.
1. Fishes – Juvenile literature. [1. Fishes.] I. Young, Jerry, ill.
II. Title. III. Series.
QL617.2.L56   1991   597 – dc20   90-49651
ISBN 0-679-81516-3
ISBN 0-679-91516-8 (lib. bdg.)

Color reproduction by Colourscan, Singapore
Typeset by Windsorgraphics, Ringwood, Hampshire
Printed in Italy by A. Mondadori Editore, Verona

Contents

What is a fish?

Wherever there is water, there are fish. In deep oceans and high mountain lakes, fish are swimming their way through life. But don't be fooled. A lot of things that swim aren't fish, and some fish hardly swim at all.

Our wet home
There is so much water on Earth that from space the planet looks blue!

Water out

Eye

Water in

Gills

How do fish breathe underwater?
With gills! Every animal needs oxygen, and fish get theirs when water, which contains oxygen, passes over these organs.

Dorsal fin

Opening to gills

Fins
Fish don't have legs, arms, or wings. Instead, they have fins. The tail fin is used for power, and the pectoral fins for steering. The dorsal fin on the back stops the fish from rolling over in the water.

Tail fin

Pectoral fin

8

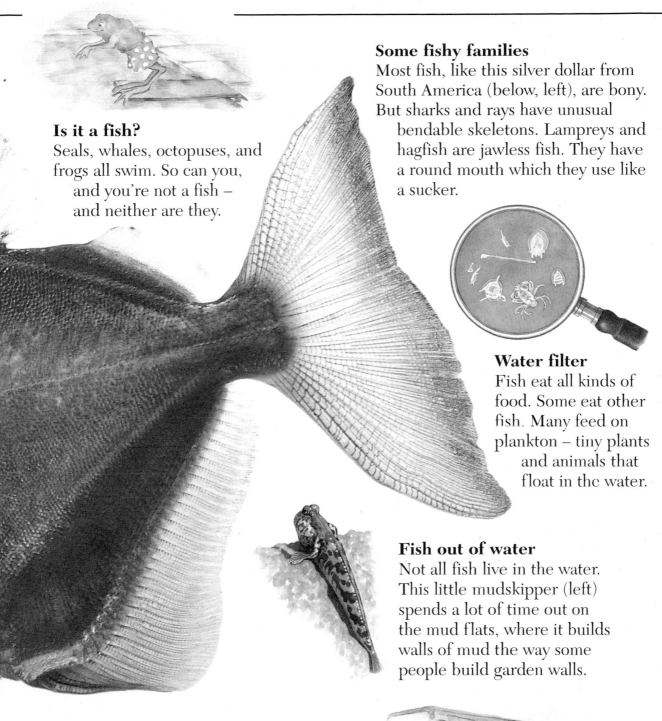

Is it a fish?
Seals, whales, octopuses, and frogs all swim. So can you, and you're not a fish – and neither are they.

Some fishy families
Most fish, like this silver dollar from South America (below, left), are bony. But sharks and rays have unusual bendable skeletons. Lampreys and hagfish are jawless fish. They have a round mouth which they use like a sucker.

Water filter
Fish eat all kinds of food. Some eat other fish. Many feed on plankton – tiny plants and animals that float in the water.

Fish out of water
Not all fish live in the water. This little mudskipper (left) spends a lot of time out on the mud flats, where it builds walls of mud the way some people build garden walls.

Convoy!
Birds get together in flocks, but fish meet up in groups called schools. One enormous school was thought to contain 3 billion herring, give or take a million!

Fishy shapes

Not all fish look like fish. Some have weird and wonderful shapes to help them hunt or hide.

Underwater trumpet
This tube-shaped hunter is a trumpetfish. It hovers head-down in the coral branches, ready to gobble up any small fish that come too close.

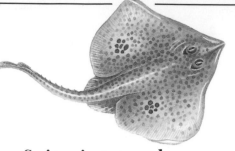

Swimming pancake
Sitting on the seafloor, the yellow-spotted stingray looks more like a pancake sprinkled with cinnamon than a fish.

Relaxed   *Disturbed*

Blown up
Like land porcupines, porcupine fish are covered with sharp spines. If you annoy this fish, its body blows up like a balloon and its spikes stick out everywhere. Enemies don't argue with that!

Packing a trunk
The elephant fish doesn't really have a trunk, but it does have a long snout for finding food.

Cowfish
It doesn't moo or chew its cud. But this tiny fish looks strangely like a cow. It swims very slowly, keeping enemies away with its long horns.

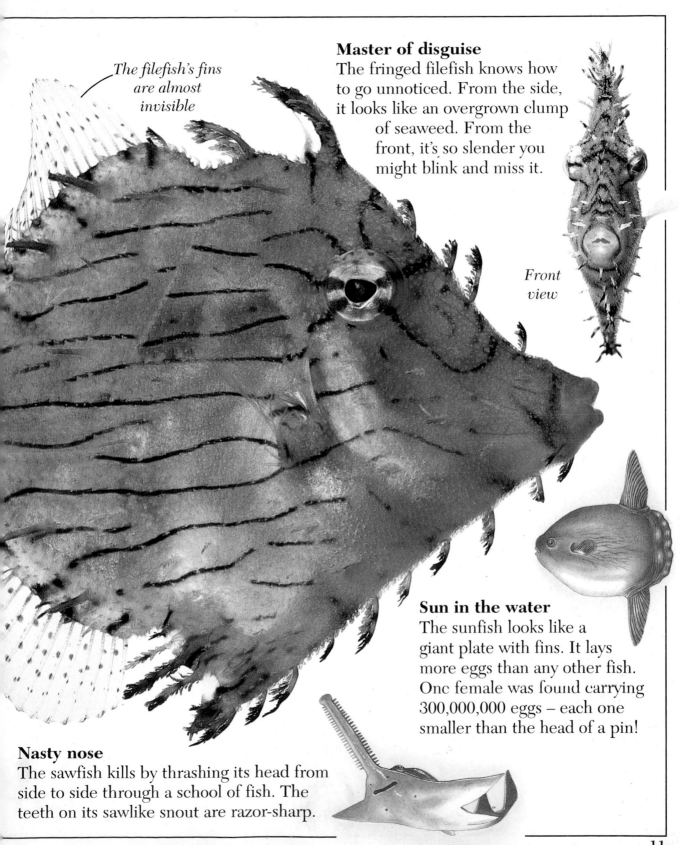

The filefish's fins are almost invisible

Master of disguise
The fringed filefish knows how to go unnoticed. From the side, it looks like an overgrown clump of seaweed. From the front, it's so slender you might blink and miss it.

Front view

Sun in the water
The sunfish looks like a giant plate with fins. It lays more eggs than any other fish. One female was found carrying 300,000,000 eggs – each one smaller than the head of a pin!

Nasty nose
The sawfish kills by thrashing its head from side to side through a school of fish. The teeth on its sawlike snout are razor-sharp.

Colors in the coral

These fabulous fish look ready for a party. But on a coral reef, their bright colors actually help them to survive.

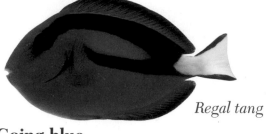

Regal tang

Going blue
A young regal tang is yellow all over. As it grows up it slowly turns blue, but its tail stays yellow.

Striped suit
Look at these fish in their smart striped suits. If you half close your eyes, it's hard to tell where they start and where they finish, which is very confusing for a hunter.

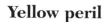

Yellow peril
Bright yellow spells danger. This boxfish looks snazzy in its dotted outfit. It is covered with poison, and a bite of its flesh could be one bite too many.

Performing clowns
Little clownfish live in the poisonous tentacles of sea anemones. Their loud colors warn trespassers to beware!

Flame angelfish

Coral garden
Brilliantly colored fish – like the flame angelfish, swallowtail angelfish, regal tang, and harlequin tuskfish – blend in beautifully in the blooming garden of a coral reef.

Swallowtail angelfish

Harlequin tuskfish

Camouflage
The tiger stripes of the harlequin tuskfish are perfect camouflage while it is out searching for food. It crunches shells and nibbles coral with its sharp teeth.

Built to kill

Sharks are killing machines. They cruise the seas sniffing out tasty morsels. Then they grab their victims in jaws like steel traps.

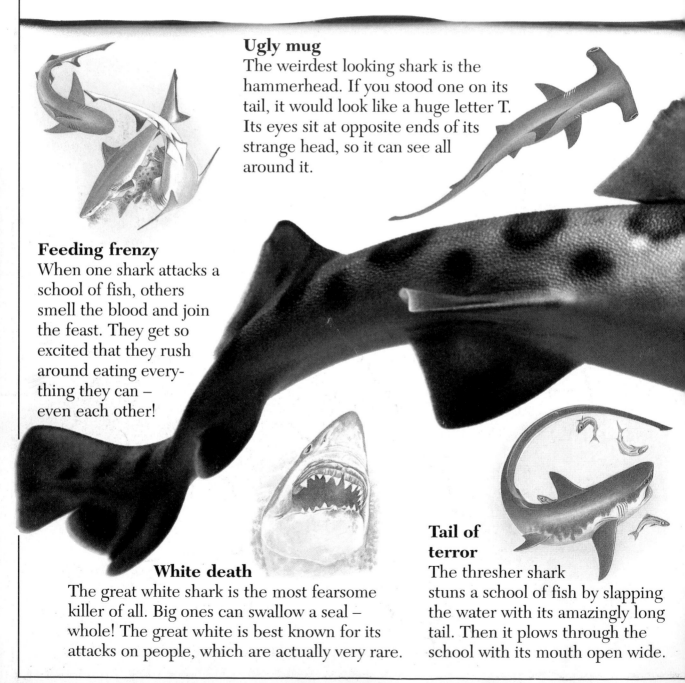

Ugly mug

The weirdest looking shark is the hammerhead. If you stood one on its tail, it would look like a huge letter T. Its eyes sit at opposite ends of its strange head, so it can see all around it.

Feeding frenzy

When one shark attacks a school of fish, others smell the blood and join the feast. They get so excited that they rush around eating every-thing they can – even each other!

White death

The great white shark is the most fearsome killer of all. Big ones can swallow a seal – whole! The great white is best known for its attacks on people, which are actually very rare.

Tail of terror

The thresher shark stuns a school of fish by slapping the water with its amazingly long tail. Then it plows through the school with its mouth open wide.

On the move
Some fish sleep the night away. But most sharks are always on the move. All that swimming keeps water flowing through their gills and helps stop them from sinking to the seafloor.

Leopard shark
There are at least 370 kinds of shark. Like most of them, this graceful leopard shark (below) swims with strong thrusts of its tail.

Jaws made of cartilage

Boneless
The shark has no bones in its body. Instead it has a skeleton made of cartilage – the same bendy stuff your ears are made of.

Huge, triangular teeth

Jaws of a blue shark

Shy shark
The wobbegong lives in the warm waters of the Great Barrier Reef, off Australia. It likes to lie on the seabed, where it looks just like a rock covered in weeds.

Slippery eels

Eels look more like snakes than fish. They wriggle through the water, and if they get stranded when their home dries out, they can even wriggle overland to a new pool.

Black ribbon eel
This beautiful fish (right) lurks in cracks and caves in the reef. When a likely meal passes by, the eel darts forward like a snake and grabs it in its toothy jaws.

Gulp!
In the depths of the ocean, food is scarce. The gulper eel has a huge mouth with elastic sides, so it can get its lips around anything it meets!

What a shock
The electric eel stuns or kills its prey with nasty shocks. It makes its electricity in special organs, like homemade batteries, which run down the side of its body.

Tweezer jaws
The snipe eel (left) also lives in deep water. It hangs around waiting for a deep-sea shrimp to pass by. The eel catches the shrimp's legs in its long jaws and eats its way up to the juicy body.

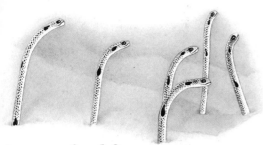

A crop of eels?
Garden eels spend most of their lives with their tails stuck in holes in the sand. They live in colonies, waving in the currents like fields of underwater wheat.

Incredible journey
When the European eel is ready to breed, it swims down its river and across the Atlantic Ocean. Then it lays its eggs off the coast of Central America – 3,400 miles from home!

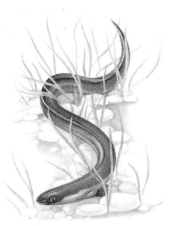

Frills on nose sense passing meals

Baby European eel

Glass eel or elver

Glass eels
Baby European eels look like see-through leaves. They float back to Europe from America on warm currents. By the time they arrive, the young eels, called glass eels or elvers, look more like adults.

The ribbon eel is a kind of moray, and like all moray eels it often sits in a crevice with only its hungry head sticking out

Meals for eels
It was very fashionable in Roman times to keep a pool of hungry moray eels. Stories tell how they were fed naughty slaves!

Hungry fish

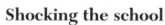

With so many hungry fish in the water, it can be a dangerous place to live.

A whale of a shark
The biggest whale shark on record weighed in at 22 tons. Most are a mere 20 tons – the same as three elephants!

Front view

Side view

Shocking the school
Barracudas need more than one fish to make a meal. They round up a whole school of fish, then they open their jaws, full of sharp, dagger-like teeth, and plow right through the middle.

Fish kebab?
Swordfish have been known to punch holes in boats by crashing into them, sword first. But they may use their swords mainly to stun the little fishes they eat by striking them.

Underwater cows
Like cows grazing in a field, parrotfish spend their days scraping algae and coral from rocks with their strong, beaklike mouths.

Healthy appetite
The oscar is a very greedy fish that lives in rivers in South America. As soon as it has attacked and swallowed one fish it starts looking for another!

Watch out for puffins!
It is not just underwater that danger lurks at mealtimes. Small fish make tasty meals for other hungry animals such as puffins.

Razor sharp
The piranha has lots of razor-sharp, triangular teeth. These fish are savage killers and a school can strip the flesh from its prey in minutes. People who fish in South America make sure they kill a piranha *before* removing the hook!

Fishy names
The oscar is also known as the velvet cichlid or the peacock cichlid.

Sea horses

If you want to ride one of these undersea ponies, you will have to shrink first. Each one is only 4 inches tall – shorter than a pencil!

Dorsal fin

Best fin forward
Most fish swim head first. But the sea horse swims with its head up and its dorsal fin rippling away like a little outboard motor.

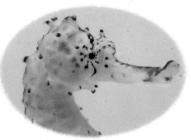

Jazzy eater
The sea horse's mouth looks like a trumpet. The little fish purses its lips and sucks in tiny creatures.

Babysitting
The male sea horse has a pouch like a kangaroo's. At breeding time, the female pops up to 200 eggs into her mate's pouch. For the next month, the babies grow safely inside.

A fishy tale
What a catch a mermaid would be! Lonely sailors have looked for these fishy ladies on long sea voyages, but none have ever been found.

Rocking horse
When it is time to "give birth," the father sea horse anchors himself to a seaweed stem and rocks back and forth to help the babies out of the pouch.

Fancy dress
You could mistake the sea dragon for a clump of seaweed. Its ragged outfit helps this sea horse hide in all the floating plants off the coast of Australia.

Tough guys
Sea horses aren't as fragile as they look. They are covered in a layer of tough plates like a suit of armor that protects them from hungry enemies.

A sea horse's eyes don't move together, so it can hunt with one eye and watch out for enemies with the other

Putting on the brakes
The sea horse has a curly tail like a monkey's. When it wants to feed or rest, it grabs a nearby piece of coral or seaweed with its tail.

Dorsal fin

Jointed bony rings

Fish with whiskers

Catfish come in all shapes and sizes, from armored midgets the size of your fingernail to prowling monsters as big as sharks!

The cat's whiskers

All catfish have whiskers, or barbels. The fish use them to gather plankton or to feel out prey on the murky bottoms of rivers and streams.

Bigmouth

For two months of the breeding season, sea catfish fathers carry 50 or more eggs in their mouths. Needless to say, they don't eat a thing until after the babies are born.

Tail fin used for propelling the fish along

Watch out – tiger!

Striped catfish go searching for shellfish in hungry gangs. Each fish is protected by three poisonous spines in its fins. A school like this in a shallow lagoon is a bundle of trouble.

Upside down

The surface of a lake may be covered with insects and small fish. The upside-down catfish has learned to swim on its back to gobble them up.

Invisible cats

The best camouflage is to be invisible. Some catfish are perfectly see-through. When they die, they turn the color of frosted glass.

Recycling

Some tropical catfish eat fruit that falls into the water. Seeds pass right through the fish and new fruit trees grow farther down the river.

Swimming in the rain

It never really rains cats and dogs, but it does rain fish! Nobody really knows why, but it seems that tornadoes suck fish up into the clouds. When the rain falls, so do the fish!

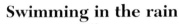

Amazonian cat

The shovel-nosed tiger catfish (above) lives in muddy rivers in the Amazon jungle. It swims around at night, finding its way (and its supper) with its long barbels.

Barbels, or whiskers

23

A fish that fishes

In the pitch-dark world at the bottom of the sea, things are not always what they seem....

The angler's "bait" is a fin that is specially adapted to look like a worm

Hiding on the seafloor

The anglerfish sits on the seabed looking like a rock. The only part of its body that other fish can see is the strange fin that grows out of its forehead.

Caught in the act

Angler means "fisherman," so anglerfish means fish that fishes. The anglerfish wriggles a special fin like a worm on a hook. When a little fish comes to investigate, the angler gobbles it up.

Light in the darkness

Angler fish that live in the darkest depths of the ocean make their own light! Little fish are attracted to the light at the end of the "worm" which dangles in front of the angler's hungry mouth.

Love at first bite

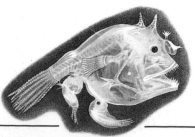

When a male deep-sea angler bumps into a female, he sinks his teeth into her. He stays attached to her body for the rest of his life, feeding from her blood like a parasite.

Trick of the lights

The deep-sea viper fish also makes its own light to lure unwary fish. Needle-sharp teeth stab the fish, and movable teeth in the throat then grab the fish and pull it into the stomach.

Pop goes the angler

The deeper you go in the sea, the heavier all that water becomes. Many deep-sea fish are held together by the pressure of the water. If they come to the surface too quickly, they pop!

Rays

What better way to live on the seabed than to disguise yourself as a sandy pancake?

Breathing in bed

Rays have special openings by their eyes called spiracles. These swish water into the fish's gills, so it can lie on the muddy seabed without suffocating.

Seen from below

The ray's mouth is on its underside. As the ray flaps along the seabed, it sifts the mud for shellfish and crustaceans.

Tune in

The Atlantic torpedo ray stuns its prey with electric shocks of more than 200 volts. That's almost enough power to run your television set!

Gentle giant

The wingspan of the mighty manta ray (above) can be over 20 feet – about six times as far as you could jump. This huge fish feeds on nothing bigger than plankton!

Tail – used more for stinging than swimming

Lounging about

When rays take time out to eat or rest, they sit quietly on the sea floor.

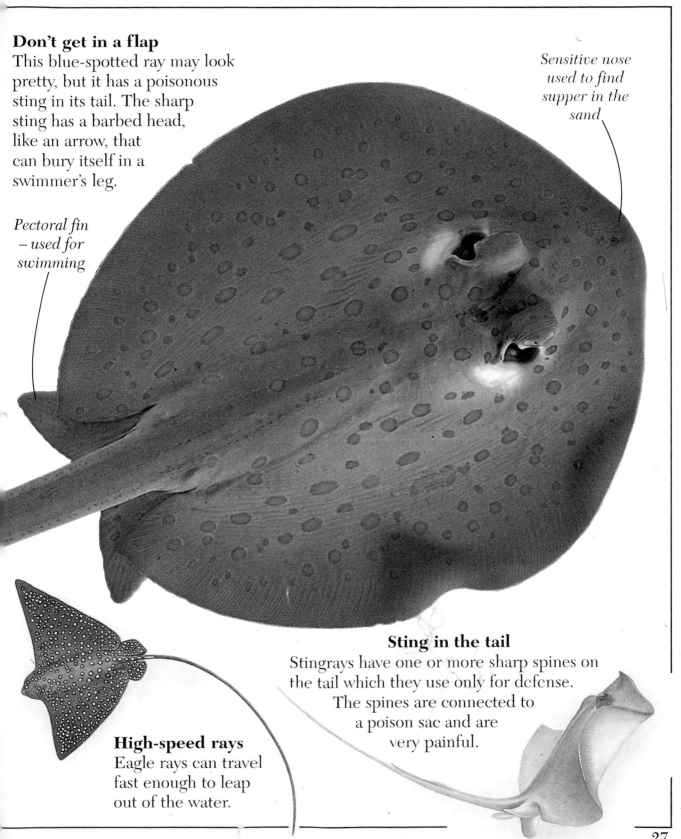

Don't get in a flap
This blue-spotted ray may look pretty, but it has a poisonous sting in its tail. The sharp sting has a barbed head, like an arrow, that can bury itself in a swimmer's leg.

Pectoral fin – used for swimming

Sensitive nose used to find supper in the sand

Sting in the tail
Stingrays have one or more sharp spines on the tail which they use only for defense. The spines are connected to a poison sac and are very painful.

High-speed rays
Eagle rays can travel fast enough to leap out of the water.

Swimming for life

Right from the start, the salmon's life is a dangerous adventure. It swims hundreds of miles to the sea, and if it survives natural and unnatural hazards, it finally goes back upriver to the stream where it was born.

1 New beginnings

Like most baby fish, young salmon hatch from eggs. The tiny, finger-sized salmon feed and swim before their long journey downriver to the sea.

2 Going home

After years in the sea, the grown-up salmon heads back up the river. It smells and tastes the water carefully to make sure that it is following the right river home. If the water is polluted, the fish may get confused and make a wrong turn.

3 Fish for food

Salmon are a useful source of food for hungry humans. Some are caught by hook and line, others are given little chance when trapped in huge nets up to 25 miles long.

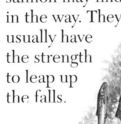

Living to lay another day

A fully grown Atlantic salmon (left) can weigh up to 60 pounds. If it is lucky it may live long enough to return upstream and lay eggs more than once.

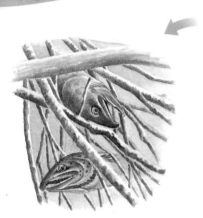

6 Final mission

Out of 3,000 eggs, fewer than fifty salmon may make it back home. Those that do, mate and lay their eggs. Then, their job done, many of the exhausted males drift off and die.

5 Leaping the falls

The trip upriver is harder than the trip down. The salmon may find a waterfall in the way. They usually have the strength to leap up the falls.

4 Danger above

Fish make a tasty meal for animals that live by the water's edge. Returning salmon are a favorite dish for grizzly bears.

Index

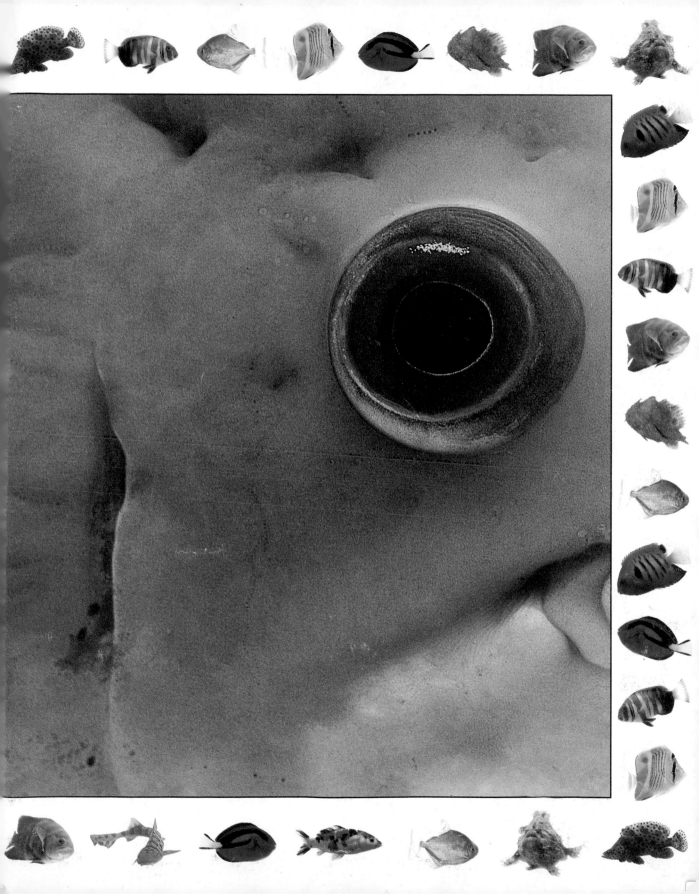